Skull Island

BY ANTHONY HOROWITZ

BOOK ANALYSIS

Written by Elena Pinaud
Translated by Oliver Brown

Skull Island

by Anthony Horowitz

ANTHONY HOROWITZ

ENGLISH WRITER

* **Born in 1955 in London**

* **Some of his works:**

    ○ *The Maltese Falcon* (1986), novel

    ○ *The Killer Photo* (2005), short stories

    ○ *Sherlock Holmes is dead. Long live Moriarty* (2014), novel

Anthony Horowitz is an English writer born in 1955. He is the author of more than forty novels, translated into many languages, and is a world-renowned writer. He is best known for his children's literature, with fantasy stories (such as *Skull Island* and its sequel, *Cursed Grail*, 1995) and crime novels (such as *The Maltese Falcon* and *Public Enemy No. 2*, 2014), which are always marked by twists and turns and a humorous style. He has also written novels for adults, such as *Moriarty* (2014), the sequel to the adventures of Sherlock Holmes, as well as scripts for television series such as *Hercule Poirot* (1991-2002) and *Inspector Barnaby* (1997-2000).

His work has won literary awards: the Polar-Jeunes prize in 1988 for *Le Faucon malté*, the European Children's Novel Prize in 1993 for *L'Île du crâne* and the Grand Prix des lecteurs du magazine *Je bouquine* in 1994 for *Devine qui vient tuer* (1991). In January 2014, he was awarded the Honorary Medal of the Order of the British Empire for 'services to literature'.

SKULL ISLAND

A MODERN FAIRY TALE FULL OF HUMOUR

- **Genre:** fantasy novel

- **Reference edition:** *L'Île du crâne*, translated from English by Annick Le Goyat, Paris, Le Livre de Poche Jeunesse, 2014, 192 p.

- **1st edition:** 1988

- **Themes:** magic, fantasy, teenage, school, vampires, wizards

Published in 1988, *The Skull Island* (*Groosham Grange* in the original version) is a sort of modern fantasy fairy tale with hints of absurdist humour. It is the story of a 12-year-old boy, David Elliot, who manages to overcome parental and school obstacles and build himself up as a teenager, with the help of a whole series of strange characters.

The ironic writing, the presence of symbols, the fine allusions to present-day society and the lively rhythm of the dialogues makes the text very rich. *The Island of the Skull was* awarded the European Children's Novel Prize of the city of Poitiers in 1993.

SUMMARY

GROOSHAM GRANGE: THE SCHOOL OF DISCIPLINE

At the end of the first term of the school year, 12-year-old David Eliot returns home with a very poor report card and extremely negative comments from his teachers. A letter informs his parents that he has been expelled, 'for constant and deliberate socialism' (p. 14). His mother, Mrs. Eliot, wishes she had no more sons. His angry father wistfully recalls the punishments his own father used to inflict on him when he did not live up to his expectations: he saw himself being 'hung by his feet in the refrigerator' (p. 10). "In my youth, I knew what discipline meant [...] The whip! That's what they're missing", he cries about today's children (p. 19). Exasperated by these poor results, he throws himself at his son with a knife: carried away by his momentum, he stabs his wife before running over her with his wheelchair and landing in the fireplace. David takes advantage of the situation to take refuge in his bedroom.

The next day, Mr. Eliot tells his wife that he wants their son to learn real discipline. At that moment, a letter seemed to grant his wish. It was a letter from Groosham Grange College offering to teach the children discipline. There, the school year has only one holiday a year and, because the school is on an island, the pupils cannot run away.

David must leave immediately for this mysterious boarding school. On the way, he meets Jeffrey and Jill, also expelled from their school and soon-to-be boarders at Groosham Grange College. The three teenagers, depressed and suspicious of the idea of entering this strange school, make a pact to help each other: they will support each other and try to escape as soon as possible. An encounter with a priest in their compartment arouses their suspicions about Groosham Grange: the man becomes frightened and faints when he hears the name of their school. And for good reason, it is in fact a school of witchcraft.

When they arrive at the station, the children are met by Gregor, the school driver who is to escort them to school. He takes them to a boat in an old hearse. At the port, Captain Baindesang, the ferryman, takes charge of them. The island of the skull impresses them above all by its wild forest and its inaccessible cliffs. The architecture of the school building is also strange: it is built in a surprising mixture of religious, administrative and ornamental styles.

FIRST MYSTERIES

As soon as he arrives, David is sent to the deputy headmaster, Mr. Kilgraw. He is keen to assure the boy that his school provides an education that is 'beyond the wildest dreams' of the students, and that the faculty is 'different' (p. 55). He tells David that he is "the seventh son of the seventh son" and that "this makes [him] special" (*ibid.*). In the meantime, David is forced to write his name in a register with his blood, which frightens him, as does the fact that he cannot see Kilgraw reflected in the large mirror in his office. This sense of dread is further heightened when he realises that the other students, all wearing black rings similar to Kilgraw's, are showing up with names that don't match the ones on their uniform labels. Nevertheless, the classes go on quite well.

David, who wonders about the nature of the school, notices a series of strange facts: Mr. Leloup keeps a dead pigeon in his locker; the kitchen looks like a biology laboratory and, at night, the other students disappear without a trace. He later realises that the teaching staff is made up of fantastic creatures: Mr. Kilgraw, the Latin teacher, is a vampire; Mr. Creer, the modelling teacher, is an undead; Mr. Leloup, the French teacher, is a werewolf; Mrs. Pedicure, in charge of the English classes, and Mrs. Windergast, the housekeeper, are witches.

Determined to get proof, David enters the office of Mr. Kilgraw, the deputy director, and burns himself on contact with a black ring kept in a drawer. Kilgraw catches him in the act and tells him that he is disappointed by his behaviour and his rebellious spirit. He hopes that one day David will be able to accept the school as it is.

Sent back to Mrs. Windergast to have his burn treated, David is offered an ointment to help him sleep better. That night, he dreams that he is with all the boarders and teachers of the college in a cave celebrating Christmas with good food, dancing and laughter. There, he sees his friend Jeffrey receiving a black ring from Mr. Kilgraw. The next morning, he finds that Mr. Kilgraw is hostile, no longer stutters and is wearing a black ring on his finger.

ATTEMPTS TO ESCAPE

Frightened, David writes a letter to his father asking him to withdraw him from the college, as he thinks the teachers want to turn him into a zombie. In exchange, he promises to fulfil his father's dream of succeeding him at the Bank of England. The boy, aided by Jill who has made several attempts to escape from the island, also decides to send bottles into the sea containing cries for help. One of them is intercepted by the Ministry of Education, which immediately sends an inspector to the island. The inspector was initially impressed by Groosham Grange. The school, having been informed of his arrival, has carefully prepared for his visit: the inspector is eventually killed by Mrs. Pedicure with a wax figure of her.

Mr. Kilgraw and his colleagues decide that it is time for David to have an interview with the school headmasters. His insubordination is interfering with their plans to make him one of them and time is running out: they plan to introduce David to magic on his thirteenth birthday. If the boy refuses, he must die. When the teenager enters the office of Mr. Fitch and Mr. Teagle, the headmasters, he discovers that they are really one and the same man with two heads. At the sight of them, he faints.

Fearing that he will be turned into a zombie, David decides to escape two days later, on his thirteenth birthday. He manages to steal Baindesang's boat and get away from the island.

Back on dry land, no one believes his story about the witches of Groosham Grange. In order to learn more about what he has just experienced, David goes to the library where he discovers the book *Black Magic in Britain*, which gives him a lot of information about the witches, their initiation and the Groosham Grange Academy of Witchcraft.

On his way out of the library, David sees the school driver, Gregor. To escape him, the boy enters the town fair and boards a ghost train. When the train comes out of the tunnel, David realises that he is on the cliffs of Skull Island. It is already his birthday: he can no longer escape them.

THE WORLD OF WITCHCRAFT

Jill appears and asks him to follow her. She reveals to David that as they are both the seventh child of a seventh child, they have special powers and the teachers only want to teach them how to use them. Together, they pass through the library mirror and find themselves in the cave that David had dreamed of at Christmas. Jill is wearing a black ring: David understands that she has just turned 13, and that this ring symbolises her initiation into witchcraft. Surrounded by teachers and students, David is faced with a dilemma: accept to forget his old identity and become a witch or be killed. The choice is quickly made.

Back for his one-day holiday with his family, David, annoyed with his parents, freezes them for three weeks with a magic spell. He then says another spell to make himself a *milkshake*, and tells himself that he is sure to pass his magic exams.

CHARACTER STUDY

DAVID ELIOT

David is a very lonely almost 13 year old, misunderstood by his teachers and parents. He has six sisters who have already left home. He is "small for his age and very thin" (p. 9), with "brown hair, blue-green eyes [and] freckles" (pp. 9-10). Lacking in self-confidence, he thinks of himself as "small and ugly" (p. 10). Sensitive and intelligent, "he possesses a [...] strength of character, [a] spirit of independence" (p. 73) which led to his expulsion from the public school his parents enrolled him in. His sense of justice and freedom prevented him from adapting to the school's "stupid rules and regulations" (p. 13). At Groosham Grange, he proves to be a good student. Alone against all odds with his friend Jill, he shows courage and perseverance. Sensing that the teachers and students are hiding a dark secret, he does not hesitate to take risks to find out what they are trying to hide from him and leads a meticulous – and dangerous – quest for the truth. This will eventually lead him to discover himself and accept his true nature: he is in fact a wizard with great powers.

EDWARD AND EILEEN ELIOT

David's parents are two caricatured characters, mean and seemingly insensitive to everything. The father, in a wheelchair as a result of his childhood abuse – which in his stupidity he finds justified and beneficial – is both verbally and physically abusive. The mother, a drinker, is subservient to her husband and supports him in his fits of authority. This is evidenced by their treatment of their son: they deprive him of dinner and Christmas, fail to listen and adopt an authoritarian attitude. There is no change in the course of the story.

JILL

Jill is a young girl on the cusp of her 13th birthday. Sent to Groosham Grange on the same day as David, she immediately becomes his ally. She has a "round boyish face, [...] short brown hair and blue eyes" (p. 31). Neglected by her ever-absent parents, she is resourceful and independent. Her rebellious nature has led her to run away from two public schools and to be expelled from the third. She is determined to escape from Skull Island, "swimming [...] if I have to" (p. 32). Once on the island, observant, brave and determined, she keeps looking for ways to leave the school and investigates with David what is really going on there. On her birthday, confronted with the truth about her witchy nature at the school's initiation ceremony, she stops resisting the world of magic.

JEFFREY

Like the two previous characters, Jeffrey is almost 13 years old and does not meet his parents' expectations.

Moreover, the fact that he is greedy, wrapped up and stammering makes him a privileged victim of mockery, except on Skull Island, where all differences are accepted. He is not a strong character, as he quickly gives in to the dark schemes of the teachers at Groosham Grange.

GREGOR

Gregor is the driver at Groosham Grange College. He is a hunchbacked, deformed and terribly ugly character who faithfully serves his employers and the pupils of the school whom he calls his 'masters' (p. 43). On his visit to the school, the Department of Education inspector congratulates Kilgraw after his meeting with Gregor: "The Academy is very sensitive to the employment of disabled people." (p. 120)

MR. KILGRAW

The vice-principal and Latin teacher is actually a vampire who fears sunlight. David finds him very old and as cadaverous and shabby looking as his office furniture. Kilgraw's job is to advocate for his college and his colleagues. He is also in charge of recruiting new students and conducting initiation rituals: he kills those who refuse to be initiated into magic and makes immortal those who agree to cooperate.

KEYS TO READING

A WONDERFULLY MODERN TALE

The narrative characteristics of the fairy tale

Skull Island is in many ways a fairy tale.

- **The narrative scheme.** The construction of the story follows that of a tale:

  - **the initial situation:** this is the beginning of the story, the moment when the setting is set and the characters are introduced; the situation is balanced, i.e. it has no reason to change.

    - David is a child who is misunderstood by his parents and has a lonely and unfulfilling childhood;

  - **the disruptive element:** this is an event that disrupts the initial situation and triggers the story itself.

    - He was expelled from school and sent to Groosham Grange on Skull Island;

  - **the twists and turns:** these are the events caused by the disturbing element and which lead to the action(s) taken by the hero to solve the problem.

    - From his arrival on the island to his escape, David has experienced several adventures such as his night visit to the school with Jill (when all the other students have disappeared) or his intrusion into Mr. Kilgraw's office during which he burns himself with the deputy headmaster's black ring before being caught;

- **the denouement:** it puts an end to the events and leads to the final situation.

  ‣ **David is magically brought back to the island and enters the world of witchcraft following an initiation ceremony;**

- **the final situation:**

  ‣ David is fulfilling his role as a sorcerer's apprentice.

- **the characters.** The characters and their relationships also bring the story closer to a fairy tale. There are:

  - **a hero:** David;

  - **adjuvants:** Jill and Jeffrey (they make a pact at the beginning of the story: 'we will stand together… us against them', p. 36);

  - **opponents:** the school staff, Captain Baindesang and other students;

Symbols and other classic elements of fairy tales

- **the number 7, a 'magic' number:** the pupils derive their magic power from being the seventh child of a seventh child;

- **the number 13, the 'evil' number: it** is at the age of 13 that the pupils of Groosham Grange are initiated and receive the black ring, a sign of their belonging to the world of magic and the evil world of the island of the skull;

- **the island:** the place where the action takes place is isolated. It is impossible to find it on a map and it is not connected to the rest of the known world. Thus, it corresponds to the indefinite places of the marvellous tales (e.g. "a very distant kingdom");

- **magical objects:**

  - the 'black ring' worn by pupils and teachers at Groosham Grange (when David touches the one he finds in Mr. Kilgraw's office, he burns himself);

  - the mirror in the library which serves as a passageway for students who pass through it every night at midnight;

  - the ointment applied by Mrs. Windergast to David's forehead, which takes him on a dreamlike journey;

  - the wax doll and the needles used to kill the inspector.

- **the wonderful characters:** Mrs. Windergast, the school's headmistress, is a witch, a typical figure in fairy tales, and Mrs. Pedicure is a witch, a typical figure in fairy tales.

Manichaeism

While traditional tales establish a clear difference between good and bad, good and evil, this story is different in that it refuses to be Manichean: the boundary between these two notions is more complex and ambiguous. In fact, in *Skull Island*, the reader realizes at the end, as does the protagonist, that the one who is believed to be 'bad' is not: David spends his time trying to escape from those who wish him well (Jill says: "We were fighting them. Yet they were on our side all along', p. 171). Moreover, it is clear that the school on Skull Island, although run by wizards and steeped in dark magic, is more pleasant than the public schools from which David, Jill and Jeffrey were expelled. David is not bored in class, makes progress in all subjects and 'there is no punishment' (p. 61). The villains, the monsters (i.e. the teachers), although gloomy and capable of giving death, are "rather nice villains" as Mr. Kilgraw points out (p. 174). It is true that the professors murdered the inspector, but they defend themselves from their crime by arguing that they had no other choice because they risked being discovered by English society. At the end of the novel, we find David blossoming, wondering whether he will choose 'white magic or black magic' and preferring to 'postpone his decision' (pp. 179-180). Finally, the traditionally evil creatures are presented here in a better light than David's parents or the English public schools, who are more the 'villains' of the story.

AN INITIATORY QUEST

A fairy tale is a story of initiation, usually involving a child who overcomes various trials to become an adult. The hero is on a quest (in this case for the truth about Groosham Grange), but it is in fact his own fulfilment that he is seeking. This is the case in this novel: young David will discover and fulfil himself at the end of the story. The ceremony he undergoes on his thirteenth birthday acts as a rite of passage to adulthood as well as an initiation into magic. The black ring he is given is the symbol of his new membership of the wizarding world. He passes from one state to another: from child to man, from mere mortal to sorcerer. This metamorphosis is underlined by the fact that he abandons his original name and takes the name of a famous former wizard (the story does not say which one he has chosen).

A FANTASTIC STORY

However, *Skull Island* is not, strictly speaking, a tale. Whereas a marvellous tale is set in an indefinite temporality ('once upon a time') and in a universe that is immediately accepted as magical, a fantastic tale is set in a realistic universe. The magical or supernatural elements that intervene are at odds with this realistic setting, that of late twentieth-century England: David does not believe in magic until he discovers the particularities of Groosham Grange and its occupants. Moreover, this school of witchcraft does everything to remain secret and hide its true nature so as not to arouse the suspicions of the population. Here are the different elements that make *Skull Island* a fantastic story:

- **fantastic creatures.** Mr. Leloup is a werewolf, Mr. Kilgraw a vampire and Mrs. Pedicure is immortal;

- **horror and terror.** The novel is not without its fright and fear, feelings often present in the fantasy genre. Some scenes are spectacular:

  - The death of Mr. Troloin, the departmental inspector, is a highlight of the story which leaves David and Jill dumbfounded, so 'terrifying is the scene' (p. 128);

  - the nightly confrontation between Jill, David and the werewolf in the thick forest of Skull Island (p. 126-127);

  - David's escape in Captain Baindesang's boat, whose torn-off hands remain hanging on the rope (p. 147);

- **references to fantasy literature.** The author plays with the codes of the fantasy novel and refers to works or authors who have marked the genre:

  - Gregor, the school's handyman, refers to Igor, the faithful servant of Frankenstein or Dracula, a typical figure in fantasy stories. He is 'horribly deformed', has 'only one eye', 'one cheek swollen, the other hollow' and 'a rare hair' (pp. 41-42). He calls the pupils his 'masters';

  - A raven watches David at the beginning of the novel as he prepares to go to Skull Island. It is probably Mrs. Windergast's pet. It is reminiscent of the famous poem 'The Raven' (1845) by Edgar Allan Poe (American novelist, playwright and poet, 1809-1849), master of the fantasy genre;

○ The novel is also a nod to *Treasure Island* (1883) by R. L. Stevenson (Scottish writer, 1850-1894), another great figure in fantasy literature. Thus the title *Skull Island* is very close to that of Stevenson's novel. The character of Captain Baindesang is part of this reference. With a 'black beard' and a 'mass of tangled hair', equipped with a sword and a 'blindfold', he wears 'a gold buckle in his left ear' (p. 46) and corresponds to the typical literary figure of the sea wolf. The narrator refers verbatim to Stevenson's work when describing the character: "You'd have thought he was straight out of *Treasure Island*." (p. 46)

A HUMOROUS NOVEL

The Skull Island is marked by the comic register which makes it a tasty hybrid novel.

The comedy of words

The story is full of puns. They can be found in:

- **the names of the characters**: Captain Baindesang, Mr. Kilgraw (*to kill* means 'to kill'), Mr. Leloup. Each refers to a salient characteristic of the character;

- **the turns of phrase**: refers to the school headmasters, who are in fact one man with two heads, the author writes: "There were two heads at the head of the school. (p. 136) Or when David's father exclaims, about his son: "For years I have been waiting for him to walk in my footsteps, at least in the footsteps of my wheelchair since I cannot walk." (p. 24)

Character comedy

Character comedy is motivated by the excessive personality of a character. The character is driven by a vice or obsession in such an excessive way that it becomes ridiculous. The character of Elliot's father, in his stupidity and excessive violence, is comic. His cartoonish penchant for discipline makes him a laughable and ridiculous character.

The comedy of gesture

The comedy of gesture, which is very common in the theatre, is based on the gestures of the characters (mimics, grimaces, falls, slaps, stumbles, etc.) which provoke the spectator to laugh. Horowitz uses it in very visual scenes, especially at the beginning of the novel, in the Eliot family: David's poor mother keeps hurting herself, either through clumsiness or through the blows her husband initially intended for her son: he runs over her with his chair, stabs her, hits her, splashes her, pushes her around…

The discrepancy and the absurd

Horowitz takes great pleasure in surprising the reader with numerous effects of rupture, of discrepancy with what is expected, which creates a comic effect. David writes in his diary about his English teacher: "Mrs. Pedicure has perfect teeth. The only drawback is that she keeps them in a glass on the corner of her desk. (p. 63) Everything in Groosham Grange takes a gloomy turn: the school vehicle is not a school bus but a hearse; the football is 'an inflated pig's bladder' (p. 65); the bursar's pet is a crow; the pupils are served not chips or cake but 'blood pudding' (p. 53) as a welcome meal. The gap thus created between what is expected of a school and the reality of Groosham Grange is comical.

A SATIRE OF SOCIETY

The Skull Island, underneath its light-hearted appearance, can be seen as a committed novel. Anthony Horowitz hides in it a criticism of self-righteous English society which he satirizes throughout the story. His messages are conveyed through humour and parodic exaggeration.

Criticism of the bourgeoisie

The bourgeoisie is represented in the novel by David's parents, who are caricatural and utterly unsympathetic. The father, a banker by profession, reads the *Financial Times*. He swears by finance and gave his son a briefcase for his eighth birthday and takes him to the stock exchange every year as a Christmas present. Obsessed with blind and violent discipline, he is insensitive and dehumanised. The mother, a housewife subservient to her husband, is stupid and has an unfortunate tendency to drink ("she poured a little glass of vodka into her cereal bowl", p. 18). The family lives in a cold, absurd and artificial world: their garden "entirely filled with plastic plants" is a perfect example (p. 28).

Criticism of public schools

Public schools are portrayed as violent, unjust and strict institutions where freedom is stifled to its last breath. The most humiliating punishments are practised: when he is expelled, they cut "David's tie in half and paint [his] jacket yellow in front of the whole school" (p. 13).

Feminism

Horowitz presents the Eliot family as the conservative family par excellence. Mrs. Eliot is bullied by her husband, who speaks badly to her and more or less inadvertently hurts her. She agrees with everything he says, but his gentle words contradict her fear of him: 'What's that, dearest?' (p. 20); 'You're probably right, dearest,' moaned Mrs. Eliot (p. 178). When David meets Jill, an independent, strong-willed girl, he cannot help but compare her to his mother and conclude that she 'dates back to the prehistoric era' (p. 31).

Moreover, the author's feminist point of view is expressed in her caricature of public schools for girls: Jill has run away from three schools where she was taught 'to make bouquets of flowers and to cook' (p. 34) and her parents sent her to Groosham Grange thinking that she will be able to 'learn manners, embroidery and such trifles' (p. 34), on the pretext that, being a girl, she should confine herself to learning domestic tasks.

The moral of the story

In this original tale, Horowitz has fun surprising the reader and plays with the codes of traditional literature. He deconstructs both the Manicheanism and the moral aspect inherent in fairy tales: he gives the villains their due in a cheerfully gloomy world. As Mr. Kilgraw says at the end of the story about the supposedly evil creatures that inhabit Skull Island: 'We've never dropped an atomic bomb, […] never polluted […] never experimented on animals or cut family allowances' (p. 173). In the end, it is the mortal world, the universe of our reality, represented in particular by David's parents, that carries the real violence within it.

AVENUES FOR REFLECTION

A FEW QUESTIONS FOR FURTHER REFLECTION...

- Can this work be described as an initiation story? Justify your answer.

- How can the Skull Island be compared with the Underworld of Greco-Latin mythology?

- What image does Horowitz portray of public schools?

- What brings this work closer to a wonderful fairy tale?

- Would you classify this work as a marvellous or fantastic story? Justify your answer.

- How is the fact that the school of witchcraft is on an island symbolic?

- How does Horowitz construct his humour and what is his aim?

- In *Cursed Grail*, the sequel to *Skull Island*, what developments occur in the character of David? Comment on David's relationship with the vampire Kilgraw.

- This work is reminiscent of *Harry Potter* (1997-2007) by J. K. Rowling (British novelist, born 1965). Compare *Skull Island* with the first book of the saga: *Harry Potter and the Philosopher's Stone*.

TO GO FURTHER

REFERENCE EDITION

HOROWITZ A, *L'Île du crâne*, translated from English by Annick Le Goyot, Paris, Le Livre de Poche Jeunesse, 2014, 192 p.

BENCHMARK STUDIES

BERGSON H., *Le Rire*, Paris, PUF, 2006, 168 p.

CHEVALIER J. and GHEERBRANT A., *Dictionnaire des Symboles*, Paris, Robert Laffont, 1969.

HOROWITZ A., *Maudit Graal*, translated from English by Annick Le Goyot, Paris, Le Livre de Poche Jeunesse, 2014, 192 p.

NOURISSIER F. and BIAISI P.-M. DE, *Dictionnaire des genres et notions littéraires*, Paris, Albin Michel, 2001.

POE E. A., « Le Corbeau », in *L'Intégrale illustrée*, Paris, Archipoche, coll. « Bibliothèque des Classiques », 2015, 850 p.

STEVENSON R. L., *Treasure Island*, Paris, Flammarion, 2010, 392 p.

ZIPES J., *The Oxford Encyclopedia of Children's Literature*, Oxford, Oxford University Press, vol. II, 2006.

Your opinion is important to us!
Leave a comment on the website of your online bookshop
and share your favourites on social networks!

Ebook EAN: 9782808686518
Paperback EAN: 9782808697910
Legal Deposit: D/2023/12603/1071

Cover: © Primento
Digital conception by Primento, the digital partner of publishers.